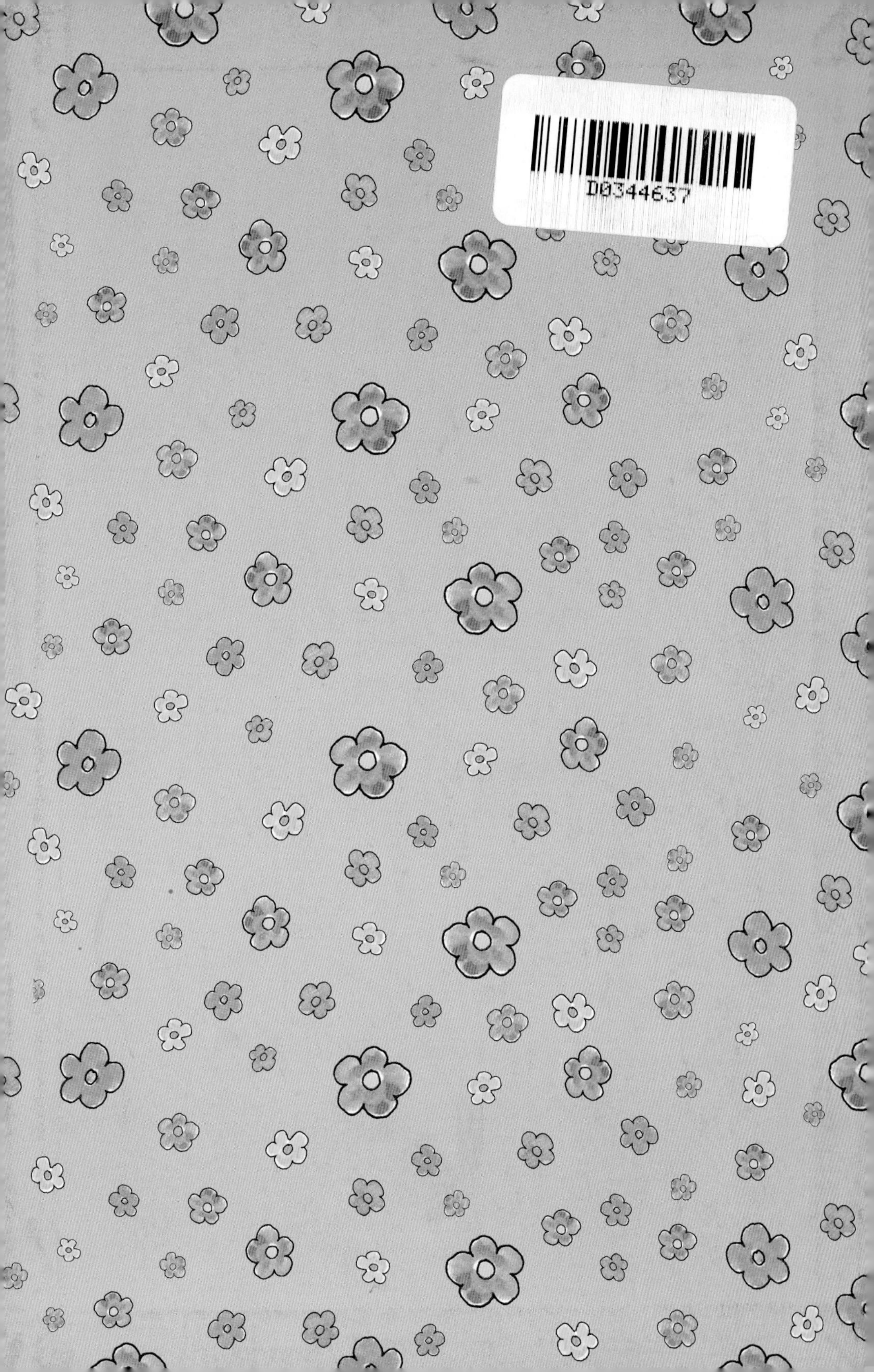
D0344637

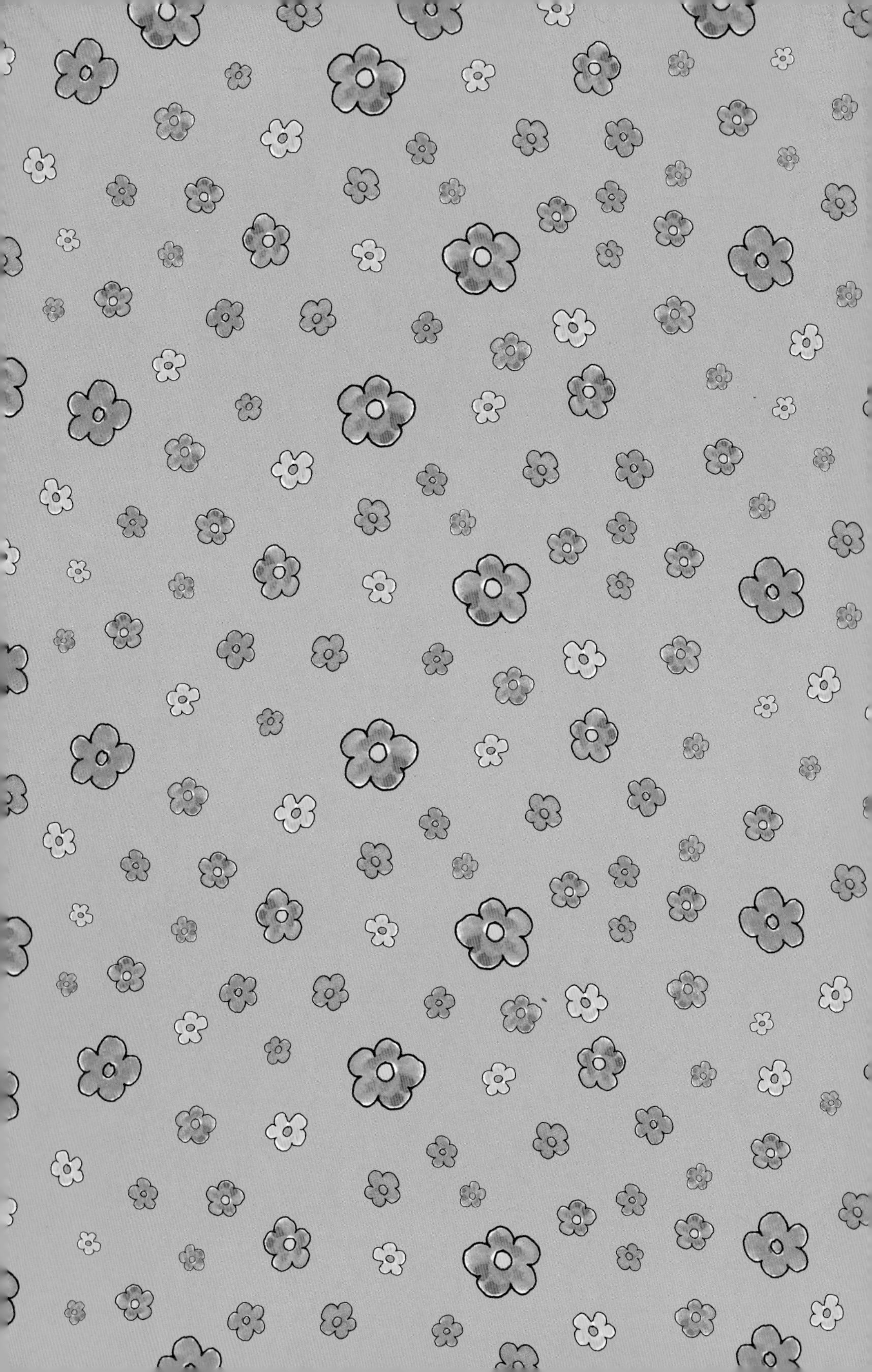

I Can Read!™
Phonics
Fancy
NANCY'S
Phonics Fun

FANCY NANCY'S PHONICS FUN

Meet Fancy Nancy
Fancy Nancy: Fancy Class!
Fancy Nancy: The Best Book Ever
Fancy Nancy: Brilliant Stars
Fancy Nancy: Robert from Paris
Fancy Nancy: Bumpy Bus
Fancy Nancy: Field Day
Fancy Nancy: Bree's Fancy Glasses
Fancy Nancy: Poison Ivy!
Fancy Nancy: Talent Show
Fancy Nancy: The Tooth Necklace
Fancy Nancy: Earth Day Rules

For information address HarperCollins Children's Books,
a division of HarperCollins Publishers,
10 East 53rd Street, New York, NY 10022
www.icanread.com

ISBN 978-0-06-233153-3

13 14 15 16 SCP 10 9 8 7 6 5 4 3 2 1

I Can Read!™
Phonics
Fancy
Nancy's
Phonics Fun

Table of Contents

Letter to Parents

Dear Parents,

Your child is about to start an exciting adventure. He or she is going to learn to read. By choosing your child's favorite characters, you have already accomplished something very important—motivation!

Fancy Nancy Phonics Fun includes twelve storybooks, planned by a phonics expert. The books are intended for children to read at home with a parent or caregiver and, eventually, by themselves.

- *Fancy Nancy Phonics Fun* introduces long and short vowel sounds. One of the key components in becoming a fluent reader is practice, so this set features one book for each sound, plus one introductory story and one book that reinforces all the sounds. Learning to read long and short vowels is rewarding because they are found everywhere!
- Fun fancy words have been included to make the stories rich and enjoyable.
- The stories also include sight words. These are words frequently found in books that can be hard to sound out. They just need to be learned by sight!
- Picture clues support the text in each story and help children learn new words.

As children master the sounds and words, they will gain experience and confidence in their ability to understand sounds, sound out words, and READ! Here are some suggestions for using *Fancy Nancy Phonics Fun* to help your child on the road to reading:

1. Read the books aloud to your child. The first time you read a story, read it all the way through. Then invite your child to follow along by pointing out words as you read them. Encourage him or her to try to sound out new words that use familiar sounds, or that are pictured in the illustrations.

2. Discuss each sound found on the first page with your child. Help your child sound out the new words in the story. Demonstrate the vowel sounds—for example, by telling your child that the **short o** vowel sound is found in the word **hot**.

3. Look at the pictures with your child. Encourage him or her to tell the story through the pictures. Point out objects in the pictures and ask your child to name them.

We hope that you and your child enjoy *Fancy Nancy Phonics Fun*, and that it is the start of many happy reading adventures.

The HarperCollins Editors

Meet
Fancy
NANCY
Book
1
Introduction
(Sight Words)

In this story, you will learn new sight words.
Can you find these words?

are	**I**	**I'm**
is	**of**	**too**

Here are some Fancy Nancy words:

adore	**cupcakes**	**dream**
family	**fanciest**	**fancy**

I’m Fancy Nancy.
I dream about being
fancy all day!

Ms. Glass is my teacher.
I adore her!
Adore is a fancy word
for love.

Bree and Robert are
my friends.

This is my family:
Mom, Dad, and my
little sister, JoJo.
We bake together.

FLOUR
Sugar

I love fancy cupcakes most of all.

My dog, Frenchy, loves fancy cupcakes, too!

Fancy Nancy

Fancy Class!

Book 2

Short a

In this story, you will read or hear words with the **short a** sound. Look for these words in the story and sound them out:

am	**class**	**fancy**
glass	**happy**	**hats**
having	**mats**	**napkin**
plan	**snacks**	**that**

Here are some sight words:

for	**look**	**looks**
my	**she**	**where**

Here are some Fancy Nancy words:

dress	**posh**	**rings**
super-duper		

My class is having a “Fancy Day.”
That makes me very happy!

I am always fancy.

I must be super-duper

fancy on Fancy Day.

I plan to wear my

fanciest dress.

My whole class looks fancy.

But where is Ms. Glass?

We make fancy place mats
and napkin rings.

We eat fancy snacks.

We make fancy hats.

Ms. Glass forgot Fancy Day.

That's OK.

We make Ms. Glass look posh.

Posh is a fancy word for fancy!

Fancy NANCY
The Best Book Ever
Book 3
Short e

In this story, you will read or hear words with the **short e** sound. Look for these words in the story and sound them out:

best	**desk**	**gets**
helped	**helps**	**kept**
next	**select**	**shelf**
them		

Here are some sight words:

about	**and**	**book**
books	**from**	**she**

Here are some Fancy Nancy words:

explorers	**Indian**	**librarian**
library	**love**	

Library Day is the best!

We select books.

Select is a fancy word for pick.

SHREK
ELOISE
A. A. MILNE
Winnie-the-Pooh
THE GIVING TREE
Alexander
ROALD DAHL
The Twits
Amelia
MADELINE
Best Reader
Narnia
THE STORY OF BABAR
Alice's
HOBBIT
DINOSAURS
MAKE WAY FOR DUCKLINGS
PURPLE CRAYON
THE STORY OF FERDINAND
Charlotte's Web
CAPS FOR SALE

The librarian helps us.
She gets us books
from the shelf.

BIG
DRAGONS

I select a book about
an Indian girl.

I read that she helped explorers.
She kept them safe.

I love the book!

I read at dinner.

I read with Dad.

I read with my doll.

SACAJAWE

I read and read until

I fall asleep . . . at my desk!

I can't wait for the next

Library Day!

Fancy
NANCY
Brilliant
Stars
Book
4
Short i

In this story, you will read or hear words with the **short i** sound. Look for these words in the story and sound them out:

big	**brilliant**	**dipper**
dizzy	**drip**	**is**
it	**lit**	**miss**
pictures	**spin**	**traffic**
trip	**will**	**windy**
with		

Here are some sight words:

going	**have**	**I**
like	**we**	

Here are some Fancy Nancy words:

planetarium	**planets**	**show**
sky	**star**	**stars**

The sky is lit up
with brilliant stars.
Brilliant is a fancy word
for shiny and bright.

I draw pictures of the stars.
The Big Dipper looks like
a big spoon.

CANCER
THE
CRAB

THE
BIG DIPPER
SUN

I spin like the planets.

I get dizzy!

VENUS

We are going on a trip
to the planetarium.
We will see a star show.
It is rainy and windy.

Drip, drip, drip!

It is raining hard.

There is lots of traffic.

We miss the show.

I have a brilliant idea.
Brilliant is also a fancy word
for really smart.
We can have our own star show.

Fancy Nancy

Robert from Paris

Book 5

Short o

In this story, you will read or hear words with the **short o** sound. Look for these words in the story and sound them out:

got	**lots**	**not**
Robert	**shot**	**soccer**

Here are some sight words:

before	**from**	**he**
how	**looks**	

Here are some Fancy Nancy words:

ami	**friend**	**Paris**
words		

Robert is a new kid in our class.

He just got here from Paris.

Paris is a fancy city in France.

I know lots about Paris.

I know lots of French words.

Robert is my *ami*.

Ami is French for friend.

RED
ROUGE
YELLOW
JAUNE
BLUE
BLEU
GREEN
VERT

Robert comes over.

We play soccer.

Robert makes a great shot!

He played soccer in Paris.

Robert looks at my poster
of the Eiffel Tower.

He has not seen
the Eiffel Tower before.

How has he not

seen the Eiffel Tower?

It is in Paris!

I am confused.

Robert tells me he is
not from Paris, France.
He is from Paris, Texas!
He is still my *ami*.

Fancy Nancy
Bumpy Bus
Book 6
Short u

In this story, you will read or hear words with the **short u** sound. Look for these words in the story and sound them out:

bump	**bumpy**	**bus**
funny	**hungry**	**lucky**
lunch	**much**	**tummy**
yuck		

Here are some sight words:

better	**but**	**her**
look	**looks**	**now**
our	**too**	

Here are some Fancy Nancy words:

museum	**shirt**

Our class is going to a museum.

I look very fancy.

Ms. Glass looks fancy, too.

The bus ride is bumpy!

We stop for lunch.

I am very hungry!

I eat a big lunch.

Back on the bus.

BUMP! BUMP! BUMP!

My tummy feels funny.

I ate too much lunch.

Stop the bus!

I get sick.

Yuck.

My tummy feels better.

But I do not look fancy now.

Lucky me!

Ms. Glass lets me wear

her shirt and hat!

Book
7

Long a

In this story, you will read or hear words with the **long a** sound. Look for these words in the story and sound them out:

anyway	**baby**	**brave**
day	**Friday**	**gained**
Grace	**great**	**hey**
makes	**may**	**maybe**
race	**rain**	**say**

Here are some sight words:

have **hear** **says** **that**

Here are some Fancy Nancy words:

field **friend** **sunny** **team**

Friday is Field Day.

I am in a race.

I am not a great runner.

I lost the race last year.

Grace is on my team.

She makes fun of me.

Grace can be mean.

I hear Grace say her baby brother runs faster than I do. That is mean.

Maybe it will rain on Friday.

But the weather says

sunny and hot.

Rats!

I have to be brave!

I tell Grace I will run

as fast as I can.

I ask her not to be mean.

We lose the race.

Grace says great job anyway!

I may have lost the race,

but I gained a friend.

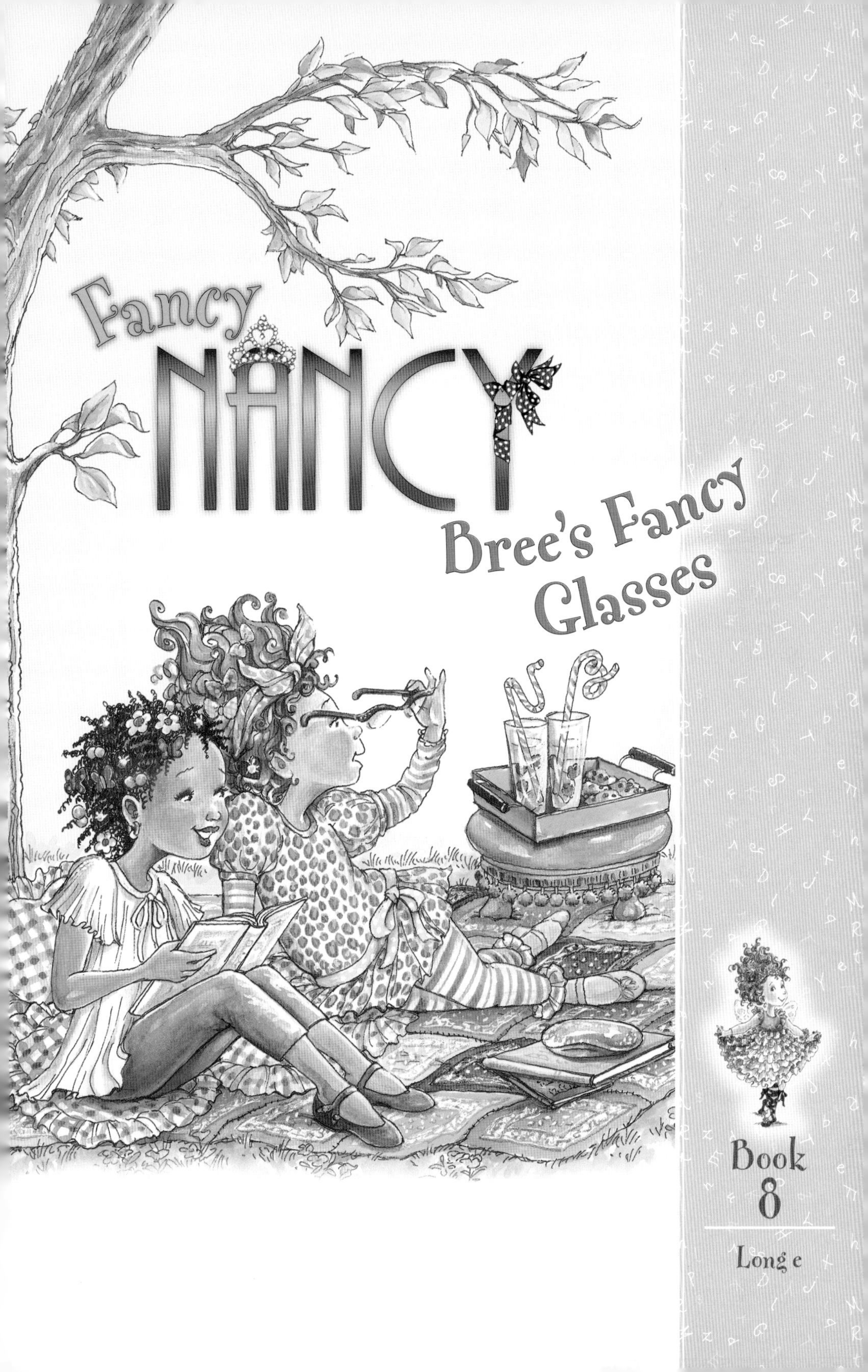
Fancy
NANCY
Bree's Fancy Glasses
Book
8
Long e

In this story, you will read or hear words with the **long e** sound. Look for these words in the story and sound them out:

be	**Bree**	**clean**
fancy	**hanky**	**keeps**
need	**see**	**seen**
she	**shiny**	**tiny**

Here are some sight words:

maybe	**now**	**they**
think	**very**	

Here are some Fancy Nancy words:

glitter	**great**	**purple**	**silver**

Bree can't see well.

She is going to the eye doctor.

Bree got eyeglasses.

Bree can see now.

She looks great.

Bree's glasses are purple
and they glitter.
I have never seen
such fancy glasses.

At the eye doctor,
Bree had to read a chart.
It had big and tiny letters.

E
FP
TOZ

Bree has a silk hankie

to clean her glasses.

She keeps the glasses
in a shiny silver case.
Glasses can be very fancy!

Hmmm. I think I can't see so well.

Maybe I need glasses, too!

Fancy
NANCY
Poison Ivy!

Nature Journal

Book
9
Long i

In this story, you will read or hear words with the **long i** sound. Look for these words in the story and sound them out:

excited	**hide**	**I**
I'm	**ivy**	**lunchtime**
my	**rhyme**	**surprise**
tiny	**wildflowers**	

Here are some sight words:

have	**our**	**out**	**watch**

Here are some Fancy Nancy words:

flowers	**gifts**	**party**
poison	**expert**	

I pick a bunch of wildflowers.

Mom says to

watch out

for poison ivy.

I know the rhyme:

Leaves of three, let it be.

I am a poison ivy expert.

We are having a surprise party
for Ms. Glass.
I will give her the wildflowers.
We hide our gifts.

DINOMITE
NANCY
BREE

At lunchtime I am so excited
that I get all itchy.
Tiny bumps are all over my face!

I have poison ivy!
I guess I'm not a
poison ivy expert
after all!

POISON OAK
POISON SUMAC
IVY

What if Ms. Glass has poison ivy?

I call right away.

No poison ivy.

Just flowers. Phew!

Fancy
NANCY
Talent Show
Book
10
Long o

In this story, you will read or hear words with the **long o** sound. Look for these words in the story and sound them out:

bold	**go**	**goes**	**hold**
home	**hope**	**jokes**	**know**
knows	**Lola**	**most**	**no**
nose	**oh**	**over**	**show**
shows	**tomorrow**	**won't**	

Here are some sight words:

have	**my**	**this**
together	**what**	

Here are some Fancy Nancy words:

dance	**perform**	**sing**
talent	**terrific**	

The talent show is tomorrow!

Lionel is my partner.

I do not know him.

What will we do for the show?

Lionel knows no jokes.

He won't sing or dance.

Oh, no!

He can hold a spoon on his nose.

But we need to perform together.

Perform is a fancy word for act.

I go over to Lionel's home.

Lionel shows me his lion toys.

He has a lot.

“Grrr!” growls Lionel.

He chases me.

This gives me hope.

I have the most terrific idea!

It's show day!

Lionel is a big, bold lion,

and I'm Lady Lola the lion tamer.

The crowd goes wild!

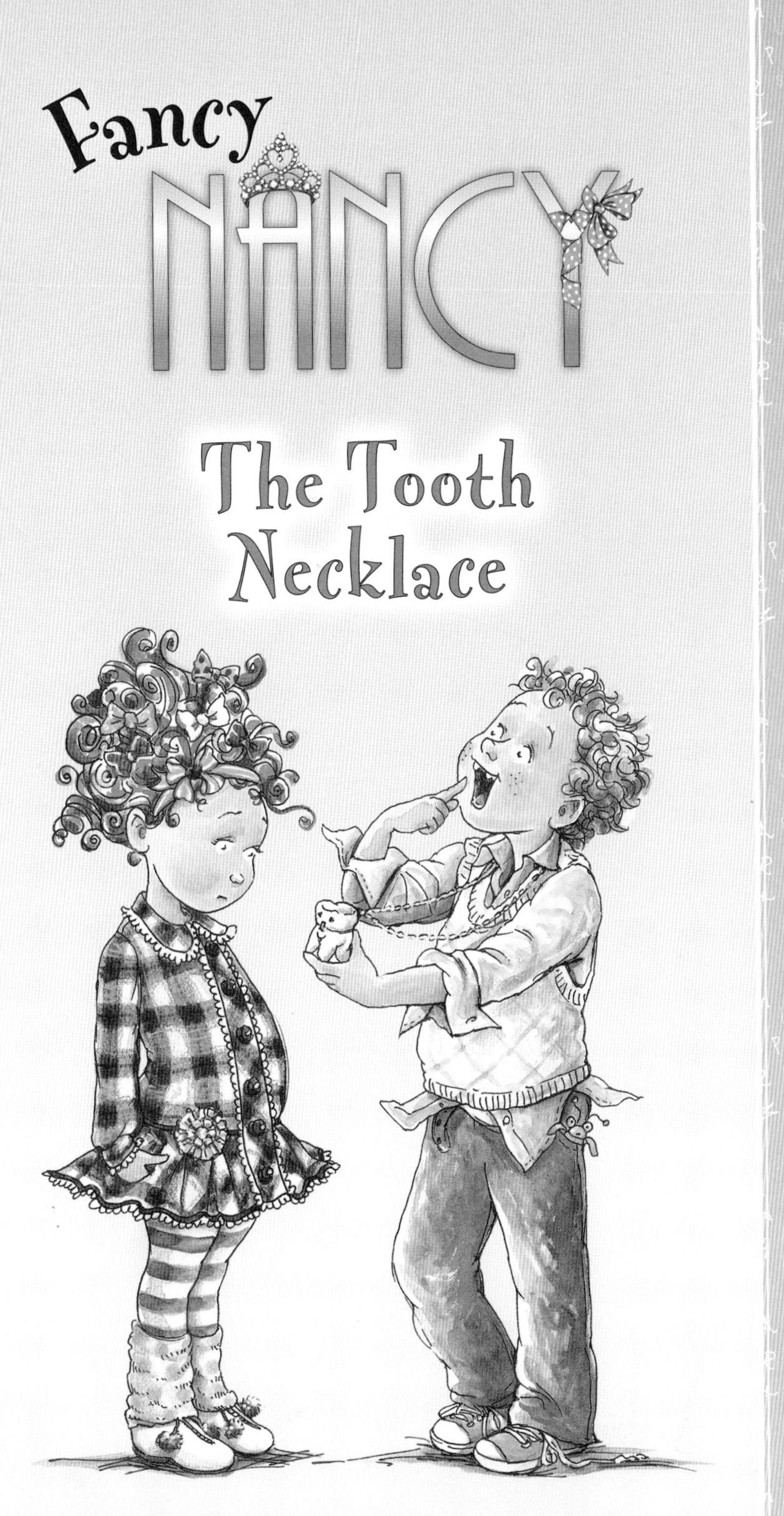

Book
11

Long u

In this story, you will read or hear words with the **long u** sound. Look for these words in the story and sound them out:

achoo	**do**	**food**
goofs	**loose**	**lose**
ooh	**school**	**to**
too	**tooth**	**you**

Here are some sight words:

around	**down**	**here**
own	**want**	

Here are some Fancy Nancy words:

long	**monkey**	**necklace**
really	**wiggle**	

Lionel goofs around on the monkey bars at school.

His head hits the bar.

Lionel jumps down.

I jump down, too.

He lost a tooth.

Ooh la la!

Lionel got a tooth necklace.

I long for one, too.

Long is a fancy word for

really, really want.

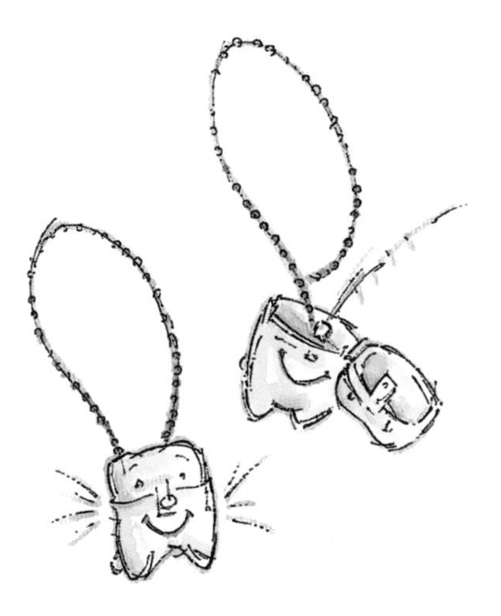

You get a necklace only if you lose your tooth at school.

I wiggle my own loose tooth.

It does not fall out.

I do NOT wiggle my tooth at home.

I eat soft food.

I do not want to lose it here.

Achoo! I sneeze on my
way to school.
Out comes my tooth.
I get a tooth necklace at school.

Fancy
NANCY
Earth Day
Rules
Book
12
Long and
Short Vowel
Review

In this story, you will read or hear words with long and short vowel sounds. Look for these words in the story and sound them out.

short vowels:

bags	**brush**	**but**	**can**
fancy	**get**	**is**	**it**
lost	**lots**	**mad**	**Mom**
napkins	**not**	**planet**	**plastic**
sweater	**will**		

long vowels:

be	**being**	**bike**	**clean**
day	**drive**	**eat**	**go**
green	**heat**	**I**	**keep**
lights	**low**	**means**	**paper**
ride	**screen**	**sees**	**she**
stay	**taking**	**teeth**	**today**
totes	**use**	**waste**	**you**

Today is Earth Day.
I love being green!
Being green means taking care
of our planet.

There are lots of green rules.

I will review them.

Review is a fancy word for go over.

Green
Rul

Rule 1: Do not drive.

Ride a bike.

Rule 2: Use totes,

not plastic or paper bags.

Rule 3: Keep the heat low.

Wear a sweater.

Rule 4: Do not waste water.

Get clean, but stay green!

Turn it off when you

brush your teeth.

Rule 5: Turn off the lights.

Turn off the computer.

Oops! Mom sees the blank screen.

She is mad.

I lost her work.

Rule 6: Eat by candlelight.

Use cloth napkins.

Guess what?

Being green can be very fancy!

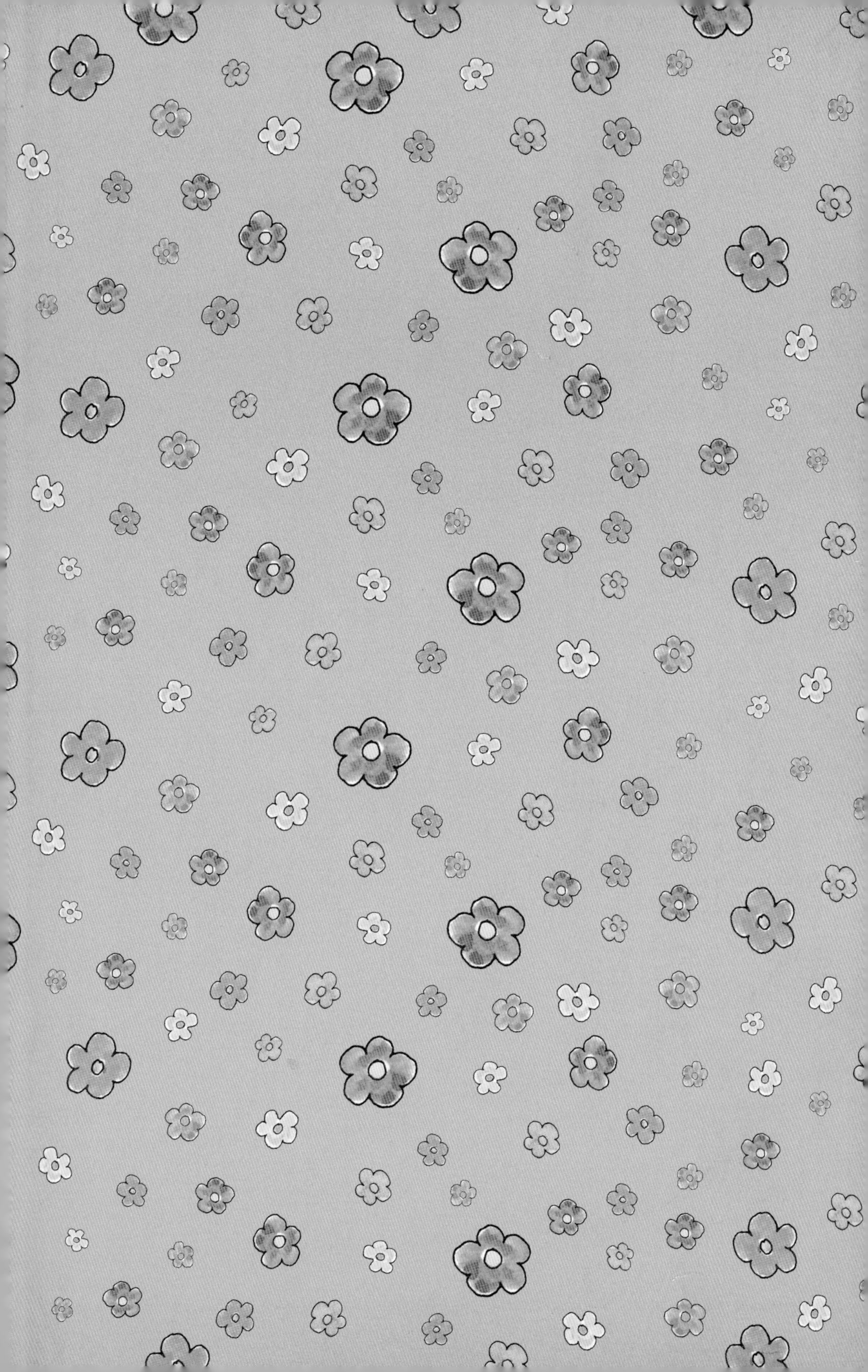

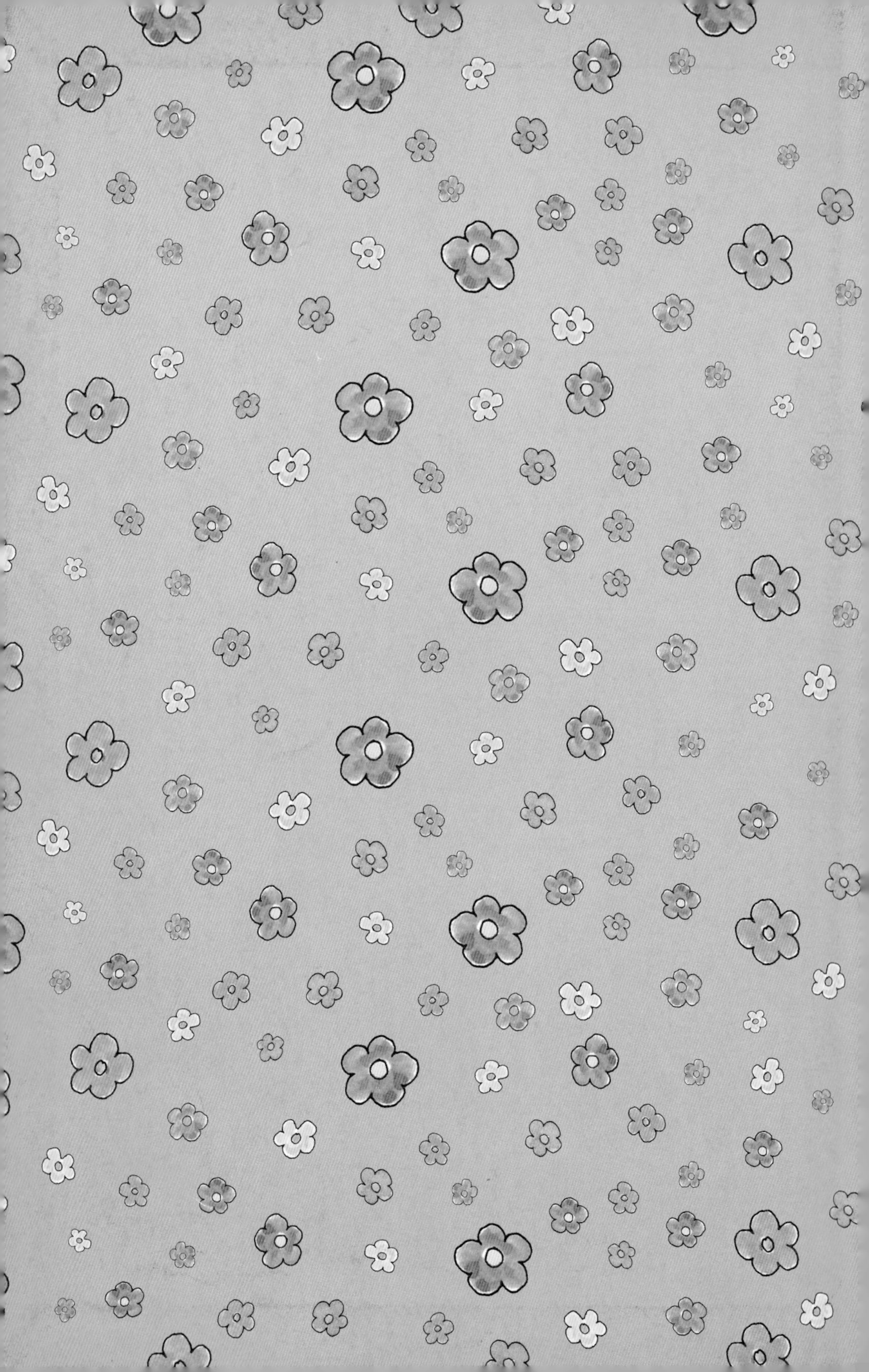